# THE LITTLE FATHER

# THE LITTLE FATHER

GELETT BURGESS

PICTURES BY RICHARD EGIELSKI

FARRAR · STRAUS · GIROUX

NEW YORK

Pictures copyright © 1985 by Richard Egielski
All rights reserved
Library of Congress catalog card number: 84-46171
Published simultaneously in Canada by Collins Publishers, Toronto
Color separations by Offset Separations Corp.
Printed in the United States of America by The Woods Group, Inc.
Bound by A. Horowitz and Sons
Typography by Cynthia Krupat
First edition, 1985

To Michael Patrick Hearn / *R. E.*

The elder Mr. Master was a big and bulky man
Before the queer event that I am telling you began;
His only son was Michael, then a little child of four,
But Michael hasn't hardly any father any more!

It was little Michael Master who detected, first of all,

That his great enormous father was becoming very small;

Now I never knew the reason, but I fancy that he shrank

Because of all the Indian ink that Mr. Master drank.

Every day, at breakfast time, when Michael tried his dad,

He found he measured something less than yesterday he had;

And still he kept on growing small and smaller every night,

Till Michael and his father were exactly of a height!

There was no Mrs. Master, so the father and the son

Got on together happily and had a lot of fun;

They wore each other's clothing, and they used each other's toys,

They became as really intimate as if they both were boys!

But Mr. Master would persist in his eccentric drink,

So littler and littler did Mr. Master shrink.

They had to cut his trousers down; and soon they were afraid

They'd have to send to Buffalo to have his long johns made.

The way he used up hats and shoes and linen shirts and ties!
As soon as they had bought them, he would need a smaller size!
But everywhere that Michael went, his father went, of course;
If Mr. Master couldn't walk, he rode on Michael's horse.

The people used to laugh at him, when they went out to walk,
For Michael's tiny father made an awful lot of talk.
The little children in the street they always used to cry,
"*I* wouldn't have a father who was only two foot high!"

But Michael was obedient to all his father told,

For though his daddy dwindled, he was forty-two years old!

And so when Michael misbehaved and tried to bite or scratch,

His father climbed upon a chair and beat him—with a match!

One day the Tax Collector called, and till he went away

The father hid in Michael's bank, because he couldn't pay.

And when to burgle Michael's bank the Tax Collector tried,

"Oh, please don't shake the bank!" said Mike, *"my father is inside!"*

One day a big policeman found him crying in the street.

"Oh, dear! I've lost my father!" little Michael did repeat;

But ere the cop could understand, he added with a smile,

"Oh, here he is! My dad was in my pocket all the while!"

And many other anecdotes do Michael's neighbors tell

Of this midget Mr. Master and his giant son as well;

Of how he swam in saucers and of how he hunted flies;

How proud he got to be about his Lilliputian size.

Soon Michael had to build a house to keep his father in,

A little paper house it was, the walls were very thin;

And when I last inquired about him, everybody said

That Michael used a microscope to put his pa to bed!